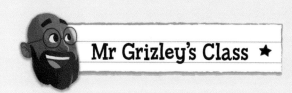

Mr Grizley's Class ★

Chad's

BIG GOAL

by Bryan Patrick Avery   illustrated by Arief Putra

raintree
a Capstone company — publishers for children

Raintree is an imprint of Capstone Global Library Limited,
a company incorporated in England and Wales having its
registered office at 264 Banbury Road, Oxford, OX2 7DY –
Registered company number: 6695582

www.raintree.co.uk
myorders@raintree.co.uk

Designed by Dina Her
Original illustrations © Capstone Global Library Limited 2024
Originated by Capstone Global Library Ltd
Printed and bound in India

978 1 3982 5276 9

British Library Cataloguing in Publication Data
A full catalogue record for this book is available from the
British Library.

CONTENTS

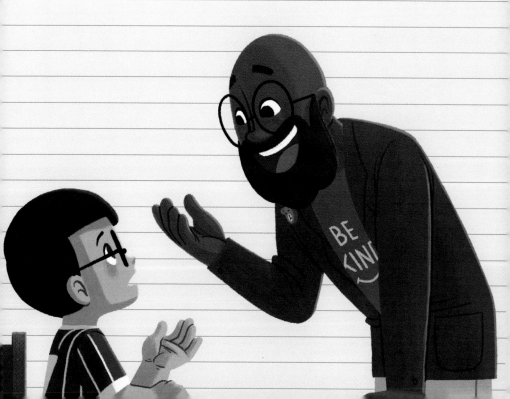

Mr Grizley's Class ★

Cecilia Gomez

Shaw Quinn

Emily Kim

Mordecai Foster

Nathan Wu

Ashok Aparnam

Ryan Clayborn

Rahma Abdi

Nicole Washington

Alijah Wilson

Suddha Agarwal

Chad Werner

Semira Madani

Pierre Boucher

Zoe Charmichael

Dmitry Orloff

Camila Jennings

Madison Tanaka

Annie Barberra

Bobby Lewis

CHAPTER 1

The task

Chad stared at the blank paper on his desk. He frowned.

"Have you finished your goal poster?" Emily asked him.

Chad shook his head. "I haven't even started."

"Here's mine," Emily said. "I'm going to learn to juggle five melons."

"Wow!" Mordecai said. "That's a lot of melons."

"I can already do four," Emily said. "One more shouldn't be too hard."

"My goal is to learn a new magic trick," Mordecai said. "It's a trick where the spectator's card keeps jumping to the top of the pack."

"That sounds cool," Chad said.

"Has everyone finished?"
Mr Grizley asked.

Chad put up his hand.
"What if I can't come up
with a goal?" he asked.

"Try to think of something," Mr Grizley said. "Any goal will do."

"But what if I can't reach my goal?" Chad asked.

"The only way you'll fail is if you don't try," Mr Grizley said.

Chad thought for a moment.

"I've got it!" he said.

CHAPTER 2

The goal

Chad scribbled on his poster. Mordecai and Emily watched over his shoulder.

"Whoa!" Emily said. "That's your goal?"

Chad held up his poster and grinned. "I'm going to run to the top of Franklin Hill," he announced.

"Franklin Hill is really tall," Madison said.

"It's so steep," Ashok said.

"I thought only bigger kids could do that," Ryan said.

Mr Grizley smiled. "I think it's a great idea," he said. "If anybody can make it up that hill, Chad can!"

Chad couldn't wait for school to end so he could go to Franklin Hill. First, though, he had a maths lesson, then reading and then science. He thought the day would never end.

When the bell rang, Chad raced out of school and across the playground. He stopped at the bottom of Franklin Hill.

Suddenly, Chad wasn't sure he could meet his goal.

"It's really tall," he said to himself. "And steep too."

Chad stared at the hill and sighed. "I'll try tomorrow," he said.

CHAPTER 3

The success

Chad went back to Franklin Hill the next day. The hill looked taller and steeper than the day before.

"I can't do this," Chad said.

"Of course you can," Mordecai said.

Chad turned and saw Mordecai and the rest of the class.

"We came to cheer you on," Nathan said.

"I really appreciate this," Chad said. "But what if I fail?"

"That's okay," Mr Grizley said, "as long as you try."

Chad took a deep breath.

"Go, Chad, go!" the class
chanted. "Go, Chad, go!"

Chad started up the hill.

Halfway up, Chad started to get tired. His legs felt heavy. His lungs burned. He wanted to stop.

"Go, Chad, go!"

Chad kept going.

"Go, Chad, go!"

Chad made it to the top. He raised his hands over his head. The class cheered.

Back at the bottom of the hill, Chad celebrated with his classmates.

"You did it," Mr Grizley said. "Great job!"

"The class was a big help," Chad said. "With everyone cheering me on, I knew I could do it."

LET'S MAKE A GOAL POSTER

Setting goals is a great way to plan for something you want to complete. Chad set a goal of running all the way to the top of Franklin Hill. You could decide that you want to read for thirty minutes each day or that you want to learn to roller-skate. We're going to create a goal poster that will help you stay on track to meet your goal.

WHAT YOU NEED:
- white or coloured paper
- coloured pens, pencils or crayons

WHAT TO DO:
1. At the top of the paper, write your name. Underneath your name, write "My goal is:" and then write your goal.

2. Picturing yourself achieving your goal can be a good way to keep yourself motivated. Draw a picture of yourself working towards, or reaching, your goal.

3. Below your picture, write down any steps you need to complete your goal. For example, if your goal is to read all the books in the

Purple Potato series, you might have a task that says, "Go to the library to get the latest Purple Potato book."

4. Once you've finished writing down your steps, put your poster up somewhere you'll see it often. This will help to keep you motivated and working towards your goal.

Of course, you can always work on more than one goal at a time. Make yourself a goal poster for each goal you want to accomplish. Here's hoping you reach your goals!

GLOSSARY

appreciate be thankful and grateful

celebrate mark a special event or moment

scribble write quickly

shoulder body part where the arm connects to the body

spectator person who watches a sport or performance

TALK ABOUT IT

1. Chad has trouble deciding on a goal for his goal poster. Why do you think he couldn't choose a goal?

2. Chad is concerned that he won't be able to complete his goal. Why does Mr Grizley say, "The only way you'll fail is if you don't try"?

3. The class's chants help Chad to reach his goal. Why do you think they helped?

WRITE ABOUT IT

1. Once he picks a goal, Chad has difficulty reaching it. His friends come to cheer him on, which helps Chad. What are some things you can do to help others reach their goals? Make a list.

2. Do you have a goal you want to complete? What is it and what help might you need to complete it? Write a paragraph.

3. Pretend Chad is your friend. Make a card to congratulate him for making his goal. Write a special message to him.

ABOUT THE AUTHOR

Bryan Patrick Avery discovered his love of reading and writing at an early age when he received his first Bobbsey Twins mystery. He writes picture books, chapter books and graphic novels. He is the author of the picture book *The Freeman Field Photograph*, as well as "The Magic Day Mystery" in *Super Puzzletastic Mysteries*. Bryan lives in northern California, USA, with his family.

ABOUT THE ILLUSTRATOR

Arief Putra loves working and drawing in his home studio at the corner of Yogyakarta city in Indonesia. He enjoys coffee, cooking, space documentaries and solving the Rubik's Cube. Living in a small house in a rural area with his wife and two sons, Arief has a big dream to spread positivity around the world through his art.